Simon Knock worked for 15 years as a postman before joining a board games company and thinking up *The Monies*. He lives in Felixstowe. Simon and John Mariani have produced the board games for *Britain's Got Talent*, *Family Fortunes* and other family favourites.

John Mariani edited *Trivial Pursuit* and went on to bring board games *Who Wants to Be a Millionaire?* and *Deal or No Deal* to the nation. He lives with his wife Sue and three sons Dario, Harry and Archie in Ipswich, Suffolk.

Michael Simpson is a freelance designer and illustrator, based in Ipswich.

Dear Pranav
Lots of Luck in your new life in America
We will miss you

First published in Great Britain in 2010 by
The Book Guild Ltd
Pavilion View
19 New Road
Brighton, BN1 1UF

Printed in Thailand under the supervision of MRM Graphics Ltd, Winslow, Bucks

A catalogue record for this book is available from The British Library.

ISBN 978 1 84624 433 9

HERE COME
THE MONIES!

Written by Simon Knock and John Mariani

Illustrated by Michael Simpson

In a busy London street sits a little old-fashioned sweet shop, which has been there for more than a hundred years. Children and adults stand and stare in wonder at the fantastic selection of treats in the window, their mouths watering.

The jars are crammed with all the old favourites, such as Black Jacks, bulls' eyes, sherbet lemons, coconut mushrooms, sweet peanuts and soft, chewy, pink shrimps.

Mr Brown, the shopkeeper, has been selling sweets for many, many years. Whatever you're looking for — fizzy cola bottles, aniseed twists, toffee bonbons or chocolate honeycomb — you are sure to find it in his shop.

At one end of the counter stands a set of old scales, which Mr Brown has used to weigh every single packet of sweets that he has ever sold.

Proudly sitting at the other end is the till, a KMS Model 43. It has a coin display at the top, which pops up each time Mr Brown presses the highly polished brass keys.

Inside the till, without anyone knowing, live The Monies. Mummy and Daddy Money are in the family room, watching television. Tenpence is in his room, looking on the Internet, and Fivepence and Tuppence are playing catch.

One day the Queen is passing by when she spots Mr Brown's sweet shop.

'Oh, Carstairs, stop! There it is. Oh, how exciting, the little old sweet shop that Nanny used to take me to. I must go in.'

The bell tinkles gently as Carstairs opens the door and the Queen walks in. She looks around at the huge array of sweets lining the walls.

'Hello, Your Majesty, lovely to see you again,' says Mr Brown.

'It's been such a long time since I last visited your shop,' replies the Queen.

'How can I help you, Ma'am?' asks Mr Brown.

'I'll have a quarter of mint imperials please, a Yorkie for Andrew, some Polos for Charles ... oh, and a gobstopper for Philip.'

'That will be £3.33 please, Ma'am,' says the shopkeeper.

'Pay the gentleman, Carstairs,' says the Queen.

Carstairs hands Mr Brown a crisp £5 note. Mr Brown presses down on the keys of the till, which gives a ring as the drawer springs open.

His hand goes into the till and picks up Daddy, Mummy, Tenpence, Fivepence and Tuppence as change. He gives them to Carstairs, who pops them into his top pocket.

The coins peep out from Carstairs' pocket, enjoying the sights on their journey.

'Where are we going?' squeals Tuppence. They soon become very excited as they see Buckingham Palace coming into view.

Once inside the sitting room of the Palace, Carstairs empties the change onto a lavish silver tray. He picks up and presses the remote control, so that the Queen and Prince Philip can watch Coronation Street. The Queen passes Philip his gobstopper and everyone settles down.

CORONATION ST.

Meanwhile, the Queen's corgis have been watching the Monies for quite some time. They can no longer contain themselves and jump up to have a closer look. The tray tips over and the coins fly everywhere.

'Quick, follow me!' says Daddy.

They run through the Palace, along wide corridors, in and out of grand rooms, with the corgis chasing close behind.

Just as the corgis are about to catch up with them, the Monies climb onto the banister and slide down.

The Monies rush out of the Palace, through the courtyard, past the guards and just make it through the iron gates.

'Phew! That was close!' says Tenpence as they take a rest in the park across the road from the Palace.

The coins don't realise that they have been spotted by Lancelot the park keeper, who comes over and picks them up.

He looks at the coins and thinks, 'Hmmm ... I've got enough here for a slice of cake to go with my afternoon tea.'

'Your usual, Lance?' asks the lady in the café.

'Yes please. I'll also have a slice of your cherry and walnut cake,' says Lancelot before he hands over the money.

The Monies are dropped into the café till and quickly huddle together in the corner.

'I'm not sure about this place, love,' says Mummy as a burly £2 coin struts past.

'Ooh, I've just stepped in some ketchup!' cries Fivepence. 'I don't like it here, Daddy.'

A lorry driver comes into the café and goes to the counter.

'Hello, I'll have a mega egg, bacon, sausage, tomato and mushroom roll, smothered in brown sauce, please ... and a big mug of tea.'

'That'll be £3.33,' says the waitress. The lorry driver hands over a £5 note. The waitress reaches into the till for the £1.67 change and picks up Daddy, Mummy, Tenpence, Fivepence and Tuppence.

The lorry driver puts the change in his pocket, then sits down to enjoy his snack.

The Monies sit squashed in his pocket while he eats his meal, then he climbs into his lorry and gets ready to make his next delivery.

The lorry arrives at a big, shiny superstore and the driver gets out to deliver a large box.

In the lorry driver's pocket, Fivepence is becoming a little mischievous.

'I'm bored,' he says, as he pulls at a loose thread.

'Don't do that!' warns Mummy. Before she can say anything else, a hole appears in the pocket.

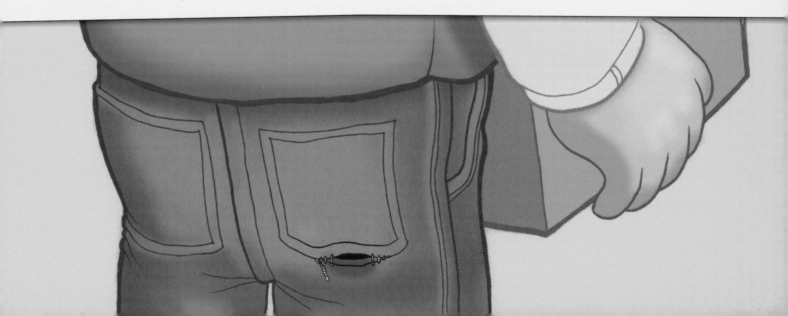

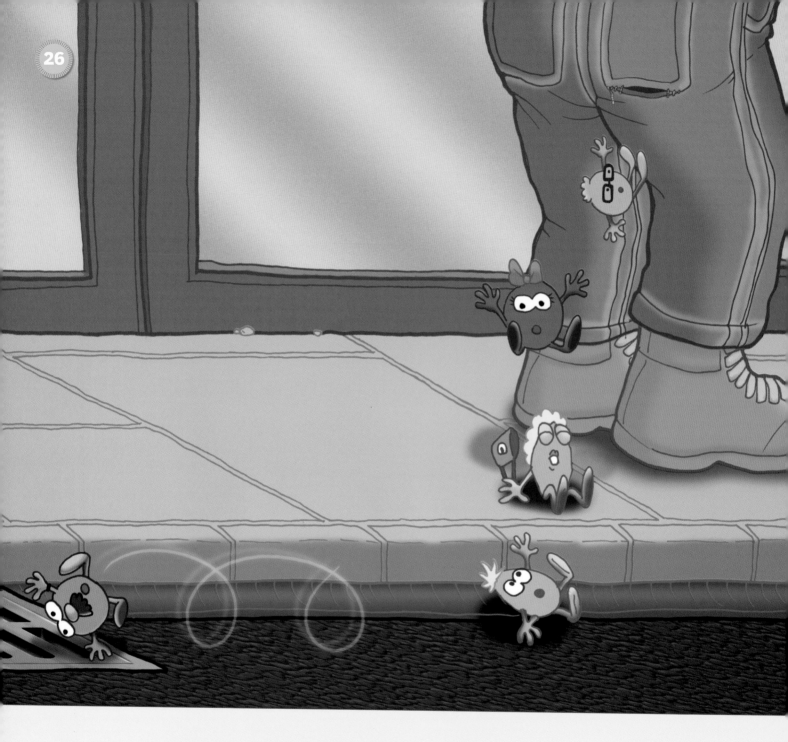

The coins tumble through the hole in the pocket
and into the gutter at the side of the road.

Daddy can't stop. He keeps rolling and rolling until he falls down the drain.

Mummy, Tenpence, Fivepence and Tuppence all race along to the drain and look down into the darkness. At first they cannot see anything...

Suddenly, they hear a voice: 'Help me! I'm on a ledge. Quick! It's smelly, slimy and dark down here.'

A little boy is walking past with his Grandad and he spots the coins by the drain.

'Look, Grandad! Someone's dropped some money,' he says. As the old man stoops over to pick up the coins he sees something shiny in the drain.

'Gosh, I can see a £1 coin down there. Give me your bubble gum, Josh.' Grandad takes the gum and presses it onto the end of his walking stick, which he then pokes around inside the drain. He manages to stick the gum to the coin, and pulls it out.

Grandad and the little boy look at the coins.

'I know,' says Grandad, 'let's go into Mr Brown's sweet shop and I'll get you some more bubble gum.'

They look all around the walls of the shop at the jars filled with colourful sweets.

The little boy chooses some golf ball bubble gum, then spots a jar of sherbet pips on the shelf behind Mr Brown.

'Look, Grandad, aren't they the ones you liked when you were a boy? Why don't you get some?'

'Oh, lovely, yes, I think I will,' says Grandad.

'That'll be £1.67,' says Mr Brown. Grandad hands over the money and the shopkeeper pops the coins into the till.

'Yippee!' shout the Monies as they are dropped back into their home.

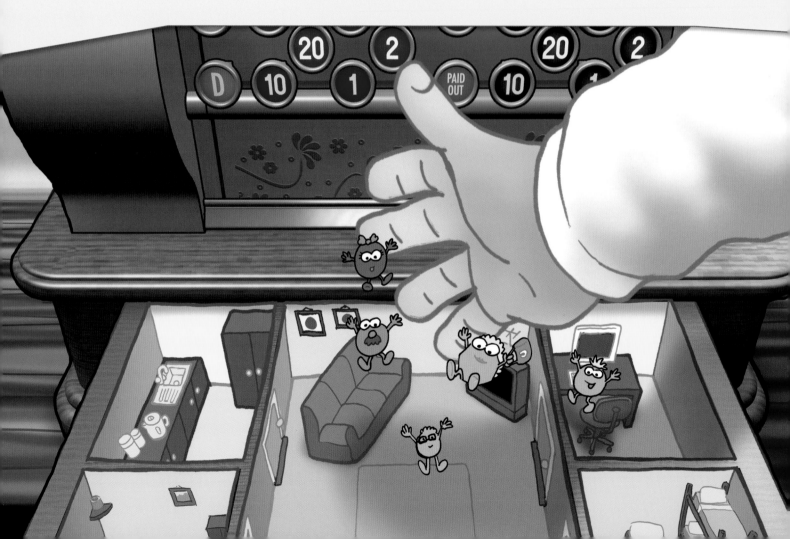

'What a day we've had,' says Daddy.
'We got to visit Buckingham Palace!'

'Yes, but it's so nice to be back home,' says
Mummy. 'Now, who would like a nice cup of tea?'

Bye-bye everyone!